A New Life - Second Edition

(The Italian Family Series)

Lucy Appadoo

Contents

1. Unchartered Territory   1

2. Broken Boundaries   14

3. Matrimony   26

4. Doubts   38

5. Seeing The Light   51

6. Close to the Edge   56

7. Danger Zone   65

8. New Journey   80

9. A Walk to the Other Side   85

ABOUT THE AUTHOR   92

ALSO BY LUCY APPADOO   94

Chapter 1

Unchartered Territory

1965

Valeria Allegro boarded the Qantas flight wearing a black shift dress that shaped her slim physique, a matching jacket, and a pair of cheap flat shoes inherited from her mother.

Her heart skipped a beat as she thought about her upcoming journey to Australia. She was leaving her family behind in Laurino, Italy. Was it her choice? Partly yes, because she wanted to leave the struggle of farm work, and partly no, because she was meeting her future husband, Roberto Morandi, whom she had yet to meet.

The marriage had been arranged by her parents and Roberto's aunt in Italy, and Valeria had ambivalent feelings about it. Would he be as handsome as his photograph? More importantly, would he be kind?

She wasn't sure if it was daring or foolish to marry a man she'd only exchanged letters with. She had doubts, of course—what woman wouldn't? But it was daring and adventurous too. She was going alone to a land where she had no job and no friends.

Her English language was far from proficient, but she hoped to establish freedom in a new country; a world filled with opportunities and possibilities.

She pushed her purse and satchel under her seat and clasped her hands in her lap. Her stomach fluttered beneath her palms, though she wasn't sure if it was from anxiety or excitement. What did an eighteen-year old know about city life? What did Valeria know about romantic relationships? Her father had forbidden her to have one. In his eyes, it was improper to have a boyfriend.

Her fists clenched at the thought of her father. He had always been strict and domineering, rarely listening to what she had to say. She'd never had a voice, and he had beaten her only to prove he was the boss. She couldn't even express her anger, as that would propel him further into brutality. What if Roberto was the same? She didn't think she could live like her mother had, constantly fearful and submissive. No, she would be different. She would defend her children.

A pang of disloyalty shot through her chest. Her mother was a gentle, nurturing woman who had done the best she could. She had taught Valeria there was nothing she couldn't tolerate and conquer. Valeria missed her already.

Across the aisle, a young man laughed and tousled his daughter's hair. Watching them, Valeria smiled. She would give anything if she and her father could have a relationship like that. But, he had mellowed over the years.

She rested back against her seat and drew a hand through her short auburn waves, thinking about her new life in Melbourne. She shivered. What if it didn't work out with Roberto? Would he respect her wishes to be her own woman?

Valeria had exchanged letters with Roberto by mail and had seen his photo, showing his good looks. He appeared friendly. It would be a marriage of convenience, a marriage in name only, and she was fine with that. All she wanted were food, shelter, and the independence to start a career in dressmaking. She could never have that independence in Laurino. There, it had been all work, all the time, as she'd helped her mother and siblings tend the small farm they called home. Each day was a struggle to feed and clothe the family, and she had little time for fun.

Breaking out of her reverie, Valeria arrived at Essendon Airport and went through customs. The clomping of feet, the indecipherable voices over loud speakers, the array of scents, and the congestion of people twisted her stomach into knots. She had never been in such a hectic space before. At home, she had always been surrounded by nature.

Valeria scanned the crowd until she spotted her future husband, Roberto. With a sigh of relief, she noted he looked exactly like his photo. She clutched her purse to her chest, hoping he wouldn't notice her quivering. He was accompanied by a young woman and a man of about the same age.

Roberto approached Valeria and gave her a stiff hug. He smelled faintly and pleasantly of woody aftershave. "Hi there, Valeria. It's good to finally meet you. How was your flight?" He kissed her on the cheek.

Valeria's heart skipped a beat. "Fine, and—aah, nice to finally meet you, Roberto."

He had vivid green eyes and jet black, wavy hair, with smiling eyes and a muscular build as if he was sporty and fit. He turned towards the woman and man beside him. "This is my sister, Angela, and her husband, Marco."

Angela gave Valeria a reserved smile and smoothed her hair. She wore it in a tight bun that enhanced her sparkling green eyes and expressive face. Serious, but attractive. She wondered if they would be friends.

She knew her mother wouldn't approve of Angela's miniskirt and loose-fitting blouse, but Valeria thought it must be the current trend in Melbourne, and she liked the look. She kissed Angela on both cheeks, feeling awkward amongst strangers and a little uncomfortable with Angela's detached air.

Marco wore pleated pants and a check shirt. He had a crew cut, blue eyes, and a robust face, giving him a warm, handsome appearance. Valeria kissed him on both cheeks too. His smile lit up the area. Valeria liked his relaxed and easy-going manner.

After picking up her luggage from the baggage claim, they headed towards the car. Roberto and Marco loaded the white Valiant with the luggage and drove to the exit, where Roberto paid a man who sat in a tiny booth. Valeria watched with interest and suppressed a smile. She'd never travelled very far outside her village until now, and the ritual seemed strange to her. It reminded her of fairy tales where trolls demanded payment in return for passage.

Roberto drove, and Valeria discovered that her new residence was in a suburb called Brunswick. She'd be living with Roberto, Angela and Marco in a house they had bought together. She didn't mind living with another couple. Their presence might distract Roberto from his marriage to Valeria. She wasn't sure she was ready to be alone with him. The thought of what he might expect from her made her mouth go dry. She didn't know what she could offer in the marriage.

Valeria fidgeted on the way to her new home, but said little. She was content listening to Angela speak about her upcoming wedding in the week ahead and the plans she had made.

She peered through the window of the car as they passed by a vast garden with overhanging trees, a lake, and large playgrounds. Women assumed to be mothers, chased laughing children. Seagulls fluttered near their feet in obvious search of food. Would she ever be as carefree as those women, as interested in their children as if they didn't have a care in the world? A yearning for family hit her deeply in the stomach as she thought about her mother, sisters and brother. She quelled another pang of guilt as she realised she didn't miss her father as much as the others.

Roberto drove into a worn, cracked driveway and stopped. Valeria had read up on Australian homes, realising the structure before her was an old classic brick house with delicate metal lace work, a pitched roof, and bay windows. It looked like a Victoriana style home, bordered by hedges, with a rose garden surrounding the house and a wide, trimmed lawn in front. A lemon tree stood at the side of the house, and the property was massive and well kept. She knew from his letters that Roberto was an avid gardener who enjoyed the outdoors. He must have been the one who maintained the garden.

As they strolled indoors, a statue of Jesus lined the mantelpiece. Paintings of Jesus and Saint Michael hung on the wall, and a mauve cotton sofa covered with a handmade crocheted blanket sat opposite. The house had a warm, cosy feel.

The display of religious items reminded her of her mother, who had prayed the rosary each evening before going to bed. Valeria smiled, remembering her mother's fingers gently touching each bead in turn.

Her mother was a religious woman, but in her own way. She always wore a cross around her neck and believed in angels and the divine. She had once told Valeria about the archangels, Saint Gabriel and Michael, and how she drew strength by praying to them. Valeria grew up believing in the strength of the angels and divine intervention, but angels also allowed free will.

During a tour of the house, Valeria flicked through a book about Italy on a tall bookshelf. She glanced through books about Australia, and a few romantic fiction novels written in Italian.

Roberto smiled as he neared her. "Feel free to read any of those books."

Valeria nodded. "Thank you." She ignored the spice of his cologne, and remembered that in his letters, he had mentioned his love of reading.

She trailed a finger along the spines and studied the titles, trying to glean something of the man who owned them. He was interested in travel, it seemed. Or did these ones belong to Angela or Marco?

She turned away and hurried through the rest of the house. There was a large living room with a television, venetian blinds that hid the sunlight, two medium-sized bedrooms, a bathroom, and an outdoor patio. The flooring was complete with plush green carpet, and the high ceilings created an illusion of space.

Roberto and Marco walked out to the back garden while Angela started cooking lunch. Valeria settled her suitcase into her room and started unpacking.

The room featured a queen-size bed and squeezed her suddenly trembling hands into fists. Her mind raced with the implications. But spotting a mattress beside the bed made her breathe a sigh of relief. Roberto obviously planned to sleep on the mattress.

Valeria placed clothing in the drawers, nightgowns and toiletries in the bathroom, and then sat on the bed with clasped hands. She closed her eyes, thinking about her new life until Angela called her out for lunch, breaking her out of her reverie.

The meal was exquisite. Back home, there had been little to eat. Her parents had struggled to feed the family, but this...this was a feast of homemade lasagne, crumbed chicken, and scalloped potatoes. Valeria felt like she was going to explode. She dabbed at her lips with the napkin and complimented Angela on the meal, steering the conversation towards her hosts. "How long have you been married?"

Angela briefly turned to her husband. "Two years. Not long, but we are planning to have children in the next couple of years."

Valeria nodded. "Nice." She beamed. "You have plenty of time to prepare for..."

A knock at the door stopped their conversation. Angela rose to answer and Valeria watched as a bulky young man entered. He had a mafia look about him, all powerful and widely-built.

Roberto got up and grabbed her hand. "Hi, Luca. This is my bride-to-be, Valeria, and, Valeria, this is Luca, our neighbour. He's from the north of Italy, and arrived a year before we did."

Valeria stepped forward, suddenly feeling uncomfortable. "Nice to meet you." She shook his hand, which lingered a moment too long.

"Likewise," he said. His deep gaze unnerved her. She averted her eyes while Angela prepared a plate of lunch for him. They all sat back down at the kitchen table, where Luca devoured his lunch and the others watched. After a few minutes, Angela brought out some fruit and walnuts to munch on.

Luca turned to Valeria. "So how do you like Melbourne so far?"

Valeria shrugged. "It seems nice and spacious." His watchful eyes seemed to penetrate her soul, continuing to unsettle her.

"Wait till Roberto shows you around. You'll love it here. As they say, 'it is the land of opportunity'."

"So they say," Valeria said. Her heart couldn't stop racing.

"Luca, are you still okay to drive Valeria to the church?" Angela asked.

"No problem," Luca said.

"Good." Angela nodded her approval. "Now, the wedding will be at St Monica's Church, and afterwards we'll have some food back here. You are coming back home, aren't you?"

Valeria picked at an orange, feeling disheartened and uneasy about this strange man being her driver. There was something about him that worried her, but then again, she didn't know the man, so how could she judge? Roberto and the others seemed comfortable enough with him.

Luca stared at Valeria. "Wouldn't miss it for the world." He then stared past her. "Roberto, my friend, you've got yourself a fine-looking woman."

"Thanks," Roberto replied, blushing.

She found out that Luca worked as an electrician, which showed in his rough, worn hands. They were hands that needed a touch of moisturiser.

The thought felt strangely intimate, and Valeria's face flushed. She looked up to find Roberto staring at her with a warm smile. What was he thinking? She hoped he wasn't getting any new ideas about their prospective marriage. She still wasn't sure he wouldn't hurt her like her father had. How could she trust him when she didn't know him? But if her parents knew his family, he must be all right. Otherwise, they wouldn't have sent her to Melbourne.

Yet...hadn't her mother thought the same thing before her own wedding? Some things were only revealed after it was too late.

Angela walked back into the kitchen and brought out a plate of store-bought panettone and minute cups of espresso coffee. Valeria had never drunk coffee. It was seen as a luxury by her parents, and they'd never been able to afford it.

When Valeria brought the cup to her lips, it was bitter and tasteless. She forced it down anyway, not wanting to be rude. It was important for Valeria to make the right impression. She tasted the panettone and enjoyed it.

She remembered her mother making the sweet bread and its deliciousness when steaming hot. The homemade version was just that tiny bit tastier than this one. It made her feel slightly homesick.

After lunch, Luca left and Valeria found her breath again. The way he had stared at her brought chills to her spine, and she wondered what his intentions were.

As Angela was washing the dishes and the men gathered outside, she turned to Valeria. "Are you okay? You look shaken up."

Valeria took a deep breath. "I'm fine."

"Luca seems to like you."

Valeria wiped the dishes thoroughly. "He doesn't even know me, but you all seem close."

"He doesn't have much of a family. His mother left him when he was a little kid. I think he was about eight at the time. He says he still remembers her."

Valeria felt a burst of sympathy for the boy Luca had once been. "And his father?"

"He said his father was pretty controlling and critical. Luca was always trying to find ways to get his approval. I think now he's quite ill in Italy, but Luca doesn't seem to care that much."

"And he doesn't have any other family?"

Angela turned the tap off and wiped her hands. "No, which is why he sticks with us. We're his family now."

Valeria had bile in her throat. Did she want him to be part of the family? Would she always feel uncomfortable in his presence? She broke out of her thoughts when Angela spoke.

"Come to think of it. You look a lot like his mother."

Valeria turned to her abruptly. "What?"

"Well, he showed us a photo of her. A photo he'd found in his father's room, which he then stole. She looks a lot like you, with the auburn hair and the pretty features."

Valeria was numb. What could she say to that? She didn't want to be a ghost of his past, but now that Angela had mentioned it, Valeria knew the idea would haunt her.

Chapter 2

Broken Boundaries

Angela arranged tulips for the church two days later. Valeria also tried on her wedding dress, which had been made by a friend of Angela's.

She wished she could have made her own dress—her mother had taught her to sew, and it had become her greatest passion—but she'd been unable to afford it. Still, she'd always brimmed with designs and had made casual clothes for her family with the use of cheap fabrics and a weathered, rusty sewing machine. She was grateful that Angela's friend had incorporated her ideas for the dress.

The dress needed slight adjustments but would be finalised by the following Saturday. It was made of organza and tulle with sequins around the waist and chest. The sleeves were three-quarter length, and layers of frills flowed outwards from the waist down, almost hoop-like.

As she sat on the sofa, she let her thoughts drift to the dream that had brought her here—her skills as a gifted seamstress would allow her to set up her own dressmaking business.

Valeria wanted to be attractive and presentable on her wedding day. Her mother had brought her up to believe that others' opinions of her mattered, and Valeria didn't like others gossiping behind her back. She wanted to make a good impression, and hoped others viewed her as strong and beautiful.

Valeria kept busy tending the back garden, tidying up the house, and cooking dinner for Roberto, Angela and Marco, who all had their own jobs. Roberto and Marco worked installing sewerage pipes, and Angela was a machine operator.

Valeria felt dull and uneducated by comparison. She'd only completed five years of primary school education in Italy before she was forced to help out her family on the farm. Still, her mother had trained her well in sewing, cooking, cleaning, and doing impeccable farm work.

She broke out of her thoughts at the sound of the doorbell. Lifting herself up, she swung open the door and shrank back when she saw Luca beaming down at her.

"Just came by to see if you needed anything." He gestured with the red metallic tool box in his hand.

It was an innocuous gesture, but something about it made her stomach clench. "No, I'm fine, thanks." As she started to push the door closed, Luca lowered his head and charged in.

"Need to put an extra power point in the bathroom. Angela said she needed one."

Valeria shook her head, hand still pressed impotently against the door panel. "Are you sure? I don't know anything about that."

"Come on. Just let me get the job done. Won't be long."

Valeria bit her lip. Maybe Angela really did need the power point, but why hadn't she told her that Luca was coming by? Through the wool in her mind, Valeria said, "Aren't you supposed to be at work?"

Luca hesitated. "Had a day off today—stuff to do. You know what it's like." He gazed at Valeria from top to bottom and moved closer. She met his gaze squarely, refusing to be intimidated by his overpowering demeanour. After a moment, he laughed and waltzed past her to the bathroom with a wild swagger.

Still feeling uneasy, Valeria followed him to the bathroom and watched him fiddle with tools. She made her way back to the kitchen, swept the kitchen floor and wiped down the bench. Engrossed in her task, she jumped when she heard his voice behind her.

"Hey there. I'm back."

Her breath catching, she turned. "Is the job done?"

He nodded. "Sure is. Good to go now. You've got an extra plug for anything you need."

She waited for him to leave, but he stood there as if transfixed by her. "You know—I wonder why you're marrying a man you don't even know. What about getting to know a man, falling in love and getting married?" A familiar fear rose in Valeria's throat. Luca frightened her as her father had, and she knew that, like her father, Luca would be quick to exploit any weakness. She needed to be strong. "We can get to know each other, Valeria. Just you and me. What do you say? I'm not so bad once you get to know me."

Valeria shook her head. "Please leave."

"Why?" He edged closer to her in the kitchen. She could smell his horrid breath. "Why should I leave? We both know you need some loving from a real man, and that man could be me." Before Valeria had the chance to move back, he closed the space between them. He stroked her face, licked his lips and stared at her in silence. Valeria felt a flutter low in her stomach. She'd never been touched the way he'd just touched her. He was almost gentleman-like.

He moved in closer to kiss her, and she finally came to her senses. This was all wrong. She stepped back, away from the kitchen, and ran to the back of the house. She heard his footsteps behind her. "Where are you going? Come back here. We were having a moment."

Valeria reached the garage outside and closed the door. Her breath came in ragged gasps and her whole body trembled. Her face felt flushed and her chest felt tight. She couldn't let him touch her. It wasn't right.

"Come on, my dear, Valeria. Come out of the garage." She cringed at the threat beneath his words. "Don't worry, I know where the key is. I'll be back."

Several minutes later, she pressed with all her strength against the door, but she wasn't prepared for the speed and strength with which he shoved it. It opened a crack, and she realised he'd found the garage key. She threw all her weight hard against the door, but his strength overpowered hers. He swung the door wide open with his leg, and she fell back, hitting her head against the concrete floor. He pulled her up and leaned in towards her.

Then he kissed her roughly on the lips. With one arm, he pinned hers against her sides, while his other hand explored her body. She craned her head away and struggled to get free.

"You bitch! What the hell are you playing at? You flirt, you tease and then you run off. Well not, anymore. I have you all to myself now."

Valeria attempted to push past him, but Luca pushed her roughly to the ground. Dazed and winded, she shook her head to clear the cobwebs and looked around for a weapon, for anything that could help her. She spotted a shovel propped against the nearest wall and stretched toward it, but Luca was faster. His face clouded with rage as he lifted the shovel above his head to strike.

Her heart raced and her vision blurred. Flashes of memory shot through her mind. Her mother's smile, her oldest sister protecting her against her father's rages. She could not have left Laurino just to die here at the hands of a madman. She kicked his leg hard, and he howled and grabbed his shin. The shovel clattered to the floor.

She rolled away, but he growled and grabbed her foot. As he hauled her towards him, she scrabbled at the floor, wincing as her nails broke against the concrete. Her breath came in quick, frightened gasps. Would he dump her body somewhere and tell Roberto she'd left him high and dry? It would be the end of her new life, the end of her dream of becoming a dressmaker. The end of everything. She couldn't let it happen. She had to save herself.

He flipped her onto her back and held her down firmly as he lay on top of her. She tried to turn her head away, but he kissed her hard on the mouth, his hands too rough as he caressed her breasts, and slid down to her hips. He tried to lift up her dress, but she shoved her right knee into his groin as hard as she could.

He gasped and fell back, cupping his crotch with his hands. "You bitch!"

Valeria pushed him away and scrambled to her feet. She sprinted out of the garage and into the house, locked the back and front doors and prayed that he would leave. Placing her hands against the door, she bowed her head and cried.

She waited until she was sure he was gone, then hobbled to the bathroom, short of breath, and washed her face. She touched the mark on her cheek where he'd slapped her, then washed off the superficial gash on the side of her head. Gazing in the mirror, she noticed her bloodshot eyes. Her skin was olive but now she looked pale in complexion. Her family's friends in Italy had always complimented her on her sparkling green eyes and full lips, but now her eyes looked dull, her lips swollen.

It would never do for Roberto to see her this way. She touched up her makeup and ran a brush through her short, auburn hair until it softly framed her face. Her heart was still racing. Her throat felt parched so she wandered over to the kitchen and poured herself water from the kitchen tap.

By the time she heard the door open several hours later, Valeria had calmed down and was resting on the sofa. Roberto came into the living room with a knitted brow, staring at her face. "What's with the bruise, Valeria? Are you okay?"

Valeria shook her head, tears springing to her eyes. "Luca—he tried to hurt me today."

Roberto looked startled. He took her hand in his and sat down on the couch beside her. "What happened?"

Haltingly, Valeria described the incident. When she was finished, Roberto shook his head. "That's ridiculous. Luca wouldn't hurt a fly. He's always helped us. He couldn't possibly do this."

Valeria's heart missed a beat, and she pressed hard on her temple. "Why don't you ask him?"

"I can't do that."

Valeria looked away, shocked and disgusted by his reaction. How could he choose not to believe her? Why would he think she'd lie about something so grave? A lump rose in her throat. "Why not?"

Roberto stared out the window. "It would create a scandal, and one we don't need with the wedding coming up. Besides, he wouldn't intentionally hurt you. He probably wanted to talk, and you running off scared him. Did he hurt you before you ran off to the garage?"

"Well—no, but I felt—felt threatened."

"But see it if from my perspective. You run off to the garage for no apparent reason. He didn't hurt you. Isn't that just a bit over the top? He just wanted to talk."

"What about him slapping me and—"

"And what?"

"He kissed me—he was—touching my breasts." Roberto's face paled. "Please believe me. He tried to rape me. If I hadn't kicked him, he would've raped me."

Roberto's jaw tightened, but he didn't answer. Moments later, Marco and Angela arrived.

"Where's dinner?" Angela asked. "You haven't cooked?"

Roberto stepped in. "Valeria claims that Luca came here and tried to attack her. Did he tell you about putting an extra power point in the bathroom?"

"He did, but I wasn't sure when he was coming."

"Well, he came today."

Both Marco and Angela angled their heads.

"That's ridiculous. Luca's been nothing but kind to us. You have to be mistaken." Angela walked off in the direction of the bathroom, and returned. "Well, there is an extra point in the bathroom and he did a pretty neat job."

Valeria clenched her fist and prayed that she could return to her homeland. What was the point of making a new life in a country with people who didn't believe in her? It was rejection all over again. Maybe it wasn't too late to return home. Could she stop this wedding?

When Roberto explained her story in detail, Angela stared at Valeria while Marco placed both hands on his wife's shoulder.

"It has to be a huge misunderstanding," said Marco.

"This is stupid," Angela said. "Why would you say this about Luca? I'm sure you misinterpreted the situation, that's all. Besides, he's never made a pass at me. He's always been the perfect gentleman. Without his help when we first settled, we would've been totally lost. He wouldn't do this."

Valeria rose from her seat. "If you don't believe me, why don't you ask Luca? See if you can tell when he's lying to you."

"I will speak to Luca," Roberto said. "I'll be right back."

"Wait up," Marco said. "I'm coming with you."

While Angela moved into the kitchen to start on dinner, Valeria went to her bedroom. She sat on the bed and pondered. She could not believe she was marrying a man she barely knew and who wouldn't support her on this. She didn't understand men at all.

Dinner was a tense affair as Valeria listened to Roberto's account of how Luca had denied attacking Valeria. "He said he kissed you on the cheek and—, then went to hug you to wish you well. Accidentally, he brushed his hand against your breast but he said he apologised and left."

Valeria's chest heaved. "How do you explain the gash and bruise on my cheek?"

"He said you fell forward accidentally, hitting your face and head on the ground. That you'd panicked for no reason."

"Only because he pushed me."

Valeria took a bite of the spaghetti bolognaise but it tasted bitter in her mouth. She sipped the homemade wine and it tasted sour. Fighting the urge to scream, she said her piece. "I think that if you guys don't believe me, there's no point in continuing."

Angela flinched. "Now, now Valeria. Let's not get dramatic. Luca's been our friend for a few years now— and we've only known you for a couple of days. Who did you think we'd believe?"

Valeria drew back, fighting tears. "But why would I lie about such a thing?"

Roberto patted Valeria's hand across the table. "We're not saying you lied. Luca was probably being friendly and you mistook that for something else."

"Are you serious?" Valeria asked. She realised that in all fairness they didn't really know her, but they had known Luca for years. He must've had a way of charming himself out of this one, which meant he'd continue to be a part of their lives. The thought of seeing him again made her stomach ache.

"Do you know how many things Luca has done for us?" Angela said. Valeria shrugged. "He helped us paint the house when we first arrived here, bought us furniture, lent us some money, and he's now helping us with the wedding. He's been a god-send."

Valeria turned away in response. It was like there were two Lucas; the one who had attacked her, and the one Angela, Marco and Roberto knew. Or thought they knew. "I'll let it go for now, but he'd better leave me alone or I won't be responsible for my actions."

The rest of dinner time was spent on small talk. Later, Valeria helped Angela with the washing up. The men smoked their cigarettes and cigars in the living room with the television switched to the Italian news channel.

Chapter 3

Matrimony

Over the next three days, Valeria kept herself securely in the house. She wouldn't risk Luca dropping in when she was on her own again. Rather, she kept herself busy by cooking, cleaning, and literally locking herself in. Luca had made her housebound.

She had shopped with Angela for the post-wedding food. Her wedding dress fit perfectly, and she was happy with the adjustments. They never spoke about the incident with Luca again, and Valeria was thankful he hadn't bothered her again. She couldn't completely blame the others for not believing her, given their long friendship with Luca, but it still hurt not to have their full support.

Valeria trembled, with a tightness in her chest on the day of her wedding. Luca had driven Roberto and Marco to the church while another friend of theirs had driven Valeria and Angela there. Originally, it was Luca who was allocated her driver, but Roberto had obviously asked someone else to do it. Perhaps he was thinking how awkward it would be for her, and she was mildly touched by the gesture.

Other close family members, including Roberto's two brothers and their wives, as well as a few friends, met at St Monica's Church in Moonee Ponds. It was a classically beautiful church with many steps leading up towards the entrance. Valeria felt numb as she took small steps outside the church, waiting for the wedding march to start playing.

It was a beautiful autumn morning, as she smelled pine-scented air and watched flocks of birds overhead. Her breathing quickened.

As she waited for Marco to walk her down the aisle, her stomach clenched and she wanted to turn back. What was she was doing marrying a man she didn't love? Was her life in Italy so bad that she needed to escape so desperately?

Valeria ignored her misgivings and focused on her surroundings. She had never viewed such a spectacular church with all those stained-glass windows, wide-open space, and such an array of candles. She'd only ever visited the much smaller church in her village.

Family members and friends sat on only one side of the church, but the other side looked. empty as it was reserved for guests of the bride. She realised how poor and lonely she felt. Everyone here seemed wealthier and more educated.

Luca winked at her from the middle pew, and her fingers tightened on her bouquet. She wondered why they had still invited him after what he'd done to her, but then again, they felt it was a huge misunderstanding. He had obviously charmed his way back into their good graces.

After the vows and signing of the documents, Roberto and Valeria strolled out of the church and stood outside while family and friends filed past with greetings and good wishes. She felt completely alone without her family present. Not that they could afford to come, but even if they were here, it wasn't like this was a real marriage. It was a marriage of convenience.

Still, Valeria couldn't help but feel a strong sense of abandonment by her parents. It wasn't the first time. Images best left buried flashed through her mind. They always surfaced under stressful circumstances such as this one.

She flashed back to one memory. It was only four years ago, when she was fourteen. Her father was having a shed built, and contractors were laying tiles on the roof. Valeria was watching the workers and running through the field. Distracted, she failed to see the plank of wood half-covered by the grass. As she crossed the plank, a protruding nail penetrated her foot and she cried out in pain.

No-one noticed, and she knew better than to interrupt her father's work. Her mother was absent for the day, so Valeria kept her injury to herself. By lunchtime, her foot was swollen and hot to the touch. She struggled to eat with her family, wincing with pain until her father impatiently asked her what the problem was. Eyes lowered, she told him about the nail. Angry she hadn't told him sooner, he sent her to the doctor by donkey on her own.

Instead, after an hour's travel, the pain felt like a razor in her foot. Her friend found her unconscious, the donkey grazing beside her, and took her to the nearby doctor. He gave Valeria a tetanus shot and said, "You were so close to dying, Valeria. It's lucky you came to see me right now—we need to fight this infection in your foot. You're a very lucky girl."

Valeria thought that if her father had genuinely cared about her safety that day, he would've taken her to the doctor himself. Instead, she'd fended for herself. If it wasn't for her friend, she could have easily died.

Breaking into her thoughts, Roberto introduced her to his friends and she kissed them on both cheeks, as was customary. When Luca came up to them, Roberto greeted him with reservation, and when he wanted to greet Valeria,

Roberto drew closer to Valeria and put his arm around her shoulder. She felt subtly protected.

With a suspicious look at Luca, Roberto said, "Why don't you bring the car around? We'll meet you there in a few minutes."

Luca's eyes darkened and his lips pursed. He nodded, turning towards Valeria with a brief sinister look in his eyes, then headed for the car park at the rear of the church.

When the well-wishers had dispersed, Roberto and Valeria climbed into the back seat of Roberto's white Valiant. Wordlessly, Luca turned the key in the ignition and turned out of the parking lot towards home. Valeria sat awkwardly in the car, lifting her dress, which had filled up part of Roberto's space. Luca stared at her in the rear view mirror so she shifted her gaze and watched the traffic. She was in awe of the shifting crowds and the vast space and roads, quite different to her own village. She'd need to adapt to the city with its dense population and busy roads.

Roberto turned to her. "How are you feeling?"

Valeria shifted awkwardly in the seat. "It all seems so unreal."

"That's natural." His hands fidgeted. "I guess tonight—aah—we'll be together." Roberto watched her curiously as if he could see right through her.

Valeria froze. How could she manage that? She looked away and didn't respond. She couldn't even decide exactly what she felt for Roberto. She liked him and realised there were many layers to his personality, but she still hardly knew him. She wasn't ready for anything sexual to happen.

She glanced up and met Luca's gaze in the mirror. His expression was one of contained anger. His hands tightened on the steering wheel, but he managed to keep his composure. Valeria felt chilled and hugged her body tight.

When they finally reached the house, Luca walked to his house next door to grab chairs for the prospective guests, while Valeria and Roberto entered the house. Her house, now too, she supposed, but that didn't feel real.

While Roberto fixed himself a drink in the kitchen, Valeria walked to her bedroom and changed into a black lace sleeveless dress she'd bought especially for the post-wedding party. She put on long, white silk gloves adorned with cream beading that went up to her elbows, and took one last look in the mirror. *Not bad.*

She breathed a sigh of relief that the wedding was over, but she was still nervous about later tonight. Well, no point worrying about that. There was still plenty to do before then.

A knock at the front door unnerved her. Was it Luca or the other guests? She practiced a quick, gracious smile in the mirror, then went out to greet the guests who had arrived.

The next hour was a blur. She chatted and smiled until her cheeks ached, then helped Angela serve an early dinner on a buffet table. The table was filled with tortellini bolognaise, baked garlic-seasoned chicken, arancini balls, salad with feta cheese, prosciutto with assorted cheeses and homemade Italian sausages with ciabatta bread.

Valeria stepped into the kitchen to grab glasses from an overhead buffet and hutch. As she placed them on a silver tray, she felt a touch on her shoulder and jumped. Luca stood beside her, grinning. She gasped and pressed her hands against her stomach so he wouldn't see them shaking. She took a long, even breath, trying to compose herself. She couldn't afford to be out of control.

"What are you doing here?" Valeria asked. She was pleased to note that her voice was steady.

Luca glanced, around, turned back to her and gently touched her face. His features softened and he stared at her as if mesmerised. "You are beautiful, you know," he whispered. "Stunning really." She glared at him, and his features hardened. Without a word, she quickly picked up the silver tray and walked out of the kitchen, facing straight ahead. "Nice butt too," she heard him say behind her. Her stomach rolled, but she forced herself to ignore him.

Eventually, Valeria ate, and found herself enjoying a conversation with two women who were talking about professional dressmakers. They had admired Valeria's wedding dress and the post-wedding dress she was wearing, mentioning a shortage of dressmakers to go around. Quite a few women were starting up their own businesses. Valeria felt a flutter of excitement. She knew she had the professional skills to do seamstress work.

She was uncomfortably aware of Luca's presence across the room. He was talking to a group of men, but his gaze never left her. When he caught her eye, he winked at her and licked his lips. Valeria ignored him and turned her focus back to her new acquaintances, but his gesture had unnerved her, and she'd missed part of the discussion. She was startled by the turn of conversation.

One of the women, Carmela, who had a warm smile, said, "My dad was so cruel. He hated it when I looked at a guy—thinking I was about to marry him. He once slapped me so hard just because I spoke to this man. He was only delivering the groceries to our home. When Dad slapped me, I fell back and almost hit my head on the cupboard behind me. Luckily for me, my mum came just in time to calm him down. He was so angry, and all I did was talk to this guy about his work." Carmela, who was petite and slim, pushed her dark bangs out of her eyes. "What's your dad like, Valeria? Was he strict like mine?"

Valeria nodded and felt her face flush. She thought of the time her father had used his belt and how she could never really talk to him. He was always angry and controlling. She couldn't shake the feeling that Luca was similar. "I guess that's all they know. My dad had a hard life, but—it's still no excuse to treat us that way."

"Too right, Valeria. I know some women who attract men just like their fathers, then they're stuck in that cycle of abuse for years. They have no self-confidence, and believe they deserve what they're getting. It's madness."

Valeria thought of her mother, who was stuck in that cycle of abuse. Her father had treated her badly, abusing her emotionally, and she took it all. Yet strangely enough he had mellowed at a later stage and was trying to change, but he still had a long way to go. Her mother had no self-confidence when it came to her father.

She was taken aback when Carmela nodded towards Luca, who was watching her from the sofa, pretending to be engaged in conversation with Roberto's brothers.

"You know, Valeria," she whispered. "You look a lot like Luca's ex-girlfriend. He seems to go for the red-head types."

Valeria drew a trembling hand through her hair. "Do I?"

Making an excuse, she rushed off into the kitchen and sipped a glass of tap water. Goosebumps lined her skin, and her heart pounded. She bowed her head and closed her eyes, wondering what she'd got herself into. She felt a lot more scared knowing that she resembled Luca's ex-girlfriend. Was that why he went after her? Or was it because she resembled his mother? Perhaps both.

She splashed cold water on her face. She was only eighteen. How could she cope with these kinds of pressures? A new husband, a strange neighbour, city life, her lack of English skills, a lack of job, and her feeling of inadequacy when it came to relationships. What had she got herself into?

Valeria wondered if Roberto would show signs of being controlling like her father and Luca. They were friends, after all, so maybe they were alike. Roberto wanted to believe that Luca was his friend and wouldn't lie to him, but he had. She already knew that Luca craved power and control, and obviously showed no respect for women. She would sympathise with any woman who had Luca as a husband.

The evening came when Marco and Angela went to bed after the guests had left. Roberto and Valeria followed suit.

She entered their small bedroom with its mahogany double bed, dresser, and two matching bedside cabinets. She closed the cream lace curtains, barely able to breathe. When Roberto started changing near the bed, Valeria rushed to the bathroom and locked the door. Belatedly, she registered Roberto's frown as he watched her hurry towards the bathroom. Would he be angry if she refused his advances?

She put on a full nightgown with long sleeves, covering her entire body to below the knees. Her hands shook as she unlocked the bathroom door, sighed and lifted the bed covers. Roberto was tucked under the covers on his side. He watched silently as Valeria slid under the covers and lay flat on her back as close to the edge of the bed as she could get. She turned off her lamp. "Goodnight." Her voice sounded thin. She could hardly hear it over the pounding of her heart.

"Are you okay?" Roberto asked.

She hesitated. "Fine. Just tired."

"So you—aah—you don't—want to—you know—."

Valeria froze again, unsure of what to say. "I'm tired. Sorry."

The silence was tense, and she wondered what Roberto was thinking. A friend back in Italy had told her about sex once, but her parents had never spoken to her about it. To them, sex was a dirty word and not a natural turn of events.

After a moment, he rolled over to face the wall. His back was stiff, the space between them both too small and suddenly immense.

Tears stinging her eyes, Valeria looked up into the darkness and listened as Roberto's breathing evened and slowed. Was this what her mother had really wanted for her? To sleep with a strange man? Or was it more her father's doing? She missed her mother terribly and wished she could be a part of this new life in Australia.

Silently, so as not to awaken her new husband, Valeria cried herself to sleep, uncertain about her new marriage. Could she ever fulfil Roberto's expectations?

Chapter 4

Doubts

One week later, Valeria started English classes, and attended her first class at a centre in Brunswick. She brought home basic English fictional texts to read while listening to the book's cassette with a tape recorder. Roberto, Marco, and Angela had started English classes a year ago and were in a more advanced class. They'd lived in Melbourne for two years and had some level of fluency.

After they returned from class, Roberto suggested taking a drive to Little Italy's Lygon Street for an espresso coffee and dessert. The breeze was noticeably cool on that autumn evening in April as Valeria strolled along the strips of restaurants and bars with Roberto, Angelo and Marco.

Valeria winced at wolf whistles and turned to see three men standing outside a restaurant staring at her. She hated being the object of their attention, her heart warming as Roberto, walked alongside her, quickly putting his arm around her shoulder. His lingering glare at the men made them turn away rapidly. Roberto smiled at Valeria, and a sudden flutter spread in her chest. She appreciated Roberto's protective streak.

They entered the Lygon Street café and got a seat close to the window. A waiter approached and Valeria ordered a baked cheesecake and a cappuccino, while the others ordered espresso coffee and the same dessert. Roberto looked at Valeria with curiosity. How are your English classes going?"

She was suddenly aware of Roberto's closeness. "Not too bad. I learned some phrases and the alphabet. I plan to listen to tapes so I can learn the language really fast."

Roberto nodded. "You'll be fluent before you know it. What are your plans once you finish your classes?"

Afraid to meet his gaze, she said, "I love sewing, so I was thinking I might get into dressmaking."

Marco looked at Angela. "Maybe you can help with that."

"Maybe," Angela said. "I'm not particularly fond of my job at the factory, so we could do something together."

Valeria nodded. This would be her dream come true. "I'd like to get a start on setting up my own business."

"I can get you in touch with the Italian women's community," Angela said. "Spread the word."

Valeria's chest lifted. "I'd like to look at doing casual wear first, and then work towards custom-made designs when I have more experience."

"Okay," Angela said. "I'll talk to my friends."

Roberto looked off into the distance. "I'd like to do an apprenticeship in carpentry. I've always loved working with my hands—making things out of wood. It's a passion of mine."

Angela smiled. "He made quite a few little knick-knacks back in Italy. Didn't you, Roberto?" Angela said.

It seemed to take some effort for him to pull his attention back to the present. "Well, it's time for me to get back to it. I just hate my job."

The wistfulness in his voice brought a lump to Valeria's throat.

The waiter's arrival with the baked cheesecakes interrupted the moment. Valeria glanced up and saw a menacing figure walk up beside the waiter. It was Luca. Two shabbily-dressed men stood behind him.

"Well hello there, guys." He flashed a broad grin. "Fancy meeting you here."

Valeria suddenly lost her appetite, unable to start on her dessert.

"Luca, man, what are you doing here?" Marco asked.

"Just here out on the town with my friends— in good old Little Italy." He stood close to Roberto, staring unabashedly at Valeria.

Angela grinned. "Anyway, thanks for your help at the wedding. You were a lifesaver."

"No worries." He smiled at Angela. "So, what are you guys doing here anyway? You don't usually go out on a weeknight."

"We just had our English class," Angela said. "Thought we'd come out and show Valeria a bit of Melbourne."

Roberto continued to eat his dessert quietly. Valeria realised he had looked up when Luca first entered but had not otherwise acknowledged Luca's presence. Was he beginning to wonder about Luca? Was Roberto finally seeing her side?

Luca nodded, his constant stares unnerving Valeria. "Sure, show her the town. Why not? Anyway, I'll catch you guys later."

Luca seated himself and his friends at a table at the other end of the café. Valeria turned away, feeling lightheaded and sick to her stomach. She needed quiet time so excused herself to the ladies' room, and Angela pointed her toward the upstairs part of the café.

It was quiet upstairs, with empty tables that could seat a large number of customers. After leaving the cubicle,

Valeria washed her hands and stared at her reflection in the mirror. Her face looked flushed, and her eyes were droopy from lack of sleep. She didn't know what to do about Roberto. Eventually he would have expectations of her as a wife, but she wasn't ready for that.

Part of it was that she simply didn't know what to expect. There were boys she'd liked back home, and one in particular was special but they'd never done more than kiss. Her father had beaten her on more than one occasion.

She kept busy with the constant, endless streams of work around the farm and house. Her life was burdened with responsibilities, and it pained her to think she'd never had much fun as a child.

A flash of movement at the edge of the mirror brought Valeria back to the present. Luca's reflection loomed in the mirror, and before she could cry out, one hand clapped over her mouth and the other pressed tightly against her breasts.

A jolt of fear ran through her. No one in the noisy café below would hear her muffled squeals. Surely, though, someone would come to check on her. Or another woman in need of the facilities would stumble in on the attack.

She squirmed and struggled as Luca pulled her roughly inside the cubicle and locking the door. She kicked him in the leg as hard as she could, but he didn't even flinch.

He slammed her hard against the cubicle door, and all the breath whooshed out of her. Before she could draw in another breath, he shoved her arms over her head and pinned her against the cubicle wall with his body. His mouth pressed hard on her own as she struggled to turn her head away. Disgusted, he leaned in and covered her mouth with his hand again.

Bile rose in her throat as his free hand explored her breasts and buttocks. He lifted her dress and pulled down her underwear, then unzipped his jeans and fumbled with the button. Frustrated, he moved his hand from her mouth and reached for his pants. Valeria screamed.

His eyes widened, then narrowed. "That scream's gonna cost you, Valeria. Mark my words, this is not over." He whirled and stormed out of the bathroom, zipping his jeans as he went.

Valeria slammed and locked the cubicle door. Then, with shaking hands, she pulled up her underwear, fixed her dress, and sank onto the toilet, shaking all over. She pressed her hand to her chest, feeling her heart thud against her palm. Tears streamed down her face, and a sob tore from her throat.

It was happening all over again. Her newfound independence was slipping away, and she felt trapped, the same way she'd been locked in by her father. Only worse, because her father had never tried to force himself on her.

She closed her eyes, trying to regroup. There must be a way to regain her freedom. She couldn't take any more of Luca's abuse. What had she ever done to deserve it? The thought that he might always have his way with her whenever he got the chance, or that he was destined to be in her life forever, sent a shudder through her. She'd always have to be on her guard.

Pressing hard on her temple, she rubbed her eyes and took a deep breath. No, she refused to be a victim. She was a survivor, and always would be.

Valeria didn't know how long she remained in the cubicle before a familiar voice broke into her thoughts.

"Valeria. Valeria, are you in there?" Angela sounded frantic. She was silent. "Valeria, I know you're in there. Are you okay?"

Valeria managed to rise from the seat and open the door. Angela stood in the gap, frowning, a question in her eyes. "What happened? You've been gone a while so Roberto asked me to check on you."

Valeria's lips trembled. Haltingly, she explained what had happened with Luca.

Angela turned her head to look around the room. "But he's not here. He left the café, so how could he have been in here?"

Valeria shook her head. "When—when did—you see him leave?"

"I didn't, but when I came up, he wasn't at his table."

Valeria pushed past her out of the cubicle, then went downstairs on wobbling knees. Luca had indeed left.

Roberto approached and laid a hand on her shoulder, looking concerned. "Is everything okay? You were gone a while."

Angela came back and motioned for Roberto to sit.

"I—I—have to go," Valeria whispered.

Roberto ignored her comment and pulled her back towards the table. "What happened in there?"

Angela gave Valeria a troubled look. "She says Luca attacked her."

Roberto's face paled and his body went stock-still. "Valeria, is that true?"

Valeria nodded.

Marco stood up to join them around the table. "Why would he do that? He's our friend, and he'd never hurt you. There's a sign of respect among us Italians."

Valeria shook her head. "He—he only left because I screamed. He didn't want to be noticed, don't you see?"

Roberto's eyes darkened. "Look, Valeria. We don't know what's happening here. You look pretty shaken up, but I still find it hard to believe that about Luca."

Valeria's voice quivered. "I know you haven't known me for long, but why would you think his words are better than mine? I have no reason to lie." She turned away, unable to hold back the tears.

"Maybe we should just talk to him," Angela said.

"Why don't we ask the staff here if they saw Luca go upstairs," Marco suggested. "We were too busy talking to notice whether he did or not."

Roberto nodded and left with Marco to meet with staff members at the bar.

Valeria was at a loss for words. Anger and fear left her disoriented. While she waited for the men to return, she took deep breaths and stared at nothing in particular. Angela tried to comfort her but she couldn't be comforted.

When Roberto and Marco returned, they both shook their heads. "I'm sorry Valeria," Marco said, "but none of the staff members at the bar noticed anything."

Roberto reached for her hand. "Look, if you want out of this marriage then just be honest."

Valeria couldn't believe what she was hearing. "So now you think I'm manipulating you— by making up this story? What, to get you to hate me so much that you'll end the marriage? That's rich. You really don't know me, do you? You really have such a low opinion of me?"

She turned and ran out of the café, passing people who stared as they ate outside on round tables alongside tall, heated lamps. She heard gentle whispers, with staff lingering outside their restaurants. They called out for her to come in and try their cuisine, but she ignored them. The blended smells of coffee, smoky pizza, and stale cigarettes made her feel ill. She didn't know where she was going, but she no longer had faith in Roberto or the others.

Valeria suddenly heard footsteps behind her, and strong arms gently grabbed her from behind. She almost tripped but somehow felt comforted by the embrace. She sobbed, knowing it was Roberto. When she turned around to face him, she fell into his arms. He stroked her hair and moved her to the side of the footpath. "Come on, let's go home and we'll talk about this."

Valeria nodded, unable to fight him. Her body and mind ached.

The drive home was quiet, and when they arrived home, Valeria noticed the lights were off at Luca's house. She trembled at the images stuck in her mind.

As Angela and Marco said goodnight to her, they gave her reassuring smiles. Did they start to believe she was telling the truth?

She knew she had no reason to lie, but why the sudden change of heart?

Valeria and Roberto sat on their double bed, and he took her hand gently. Valeria's spine tingled. She was touched by his kindness.

He spoke up first." Now I want to know exactly what happened tonight. No edits. I want the whole truth."

Valeria sighed, avoiding his gaze. She closed her eyes momentarily whilst recounting the terrorising incident. Roberto sat in silence as if processing the information. When she opened her eyes, he let go of her hand, rose from the bed and walked towards the window. He drew the curtain aside and peered into the darkness. His back was towards her and she didn't know what to make of his silence.

He drew a hand through his hair and turned back to her. "I've experienced a lot of pain and suffering in my life, but I—"

Valeria was surprised by that comment. "You what?"

"I never meant for you to come here under these circumstances. I never wanted to see you suffer as I had suffered. I know your life in Italy wasn't a picnic, but I don't want this kind of life for you. A life where you're constantly looking over your shoulder, not feeling safe."

Valeria nodded. "We'll face him tomorrow, first thing."

Roberto stood by the bed, then moved to sit beside her. He gently held her hand. "Yes, first thing tomorrow, but I will face him alone."

Valeria was silent for a few minutes. "Why do you believe me now and not the first time he attacked me?"

His thumb caressed the back of her hand. "I guess because Luca's been a friend and I didn't want to believe that about him. I didn't want to feel betrayed by someone I completely trusted. I've felt lost and alone much of my life, and I didn't want to go through that again. I'm sorry. It was my issue, and nothing at all to do with you."

"What happened to you in Italy, Roberto?"

Roberto drew back. "Nothing I wish to get into. Another time, okay?"

Valeria was aware of his deep breaths. Her chest tightened. "Sure."

He averted his eyes. "I guess seeing you at the café, I could tell you were really spooked. One minute Luca was there and the next minute he was gone. Not to mention Angela seeing how terrified you were. It was just too much of a coincidence."

Valeria smiled. "Thanks for believing in me."

"No problem." He rose and grabbed his pyjamas. "Now let's get to bed. It's been a long day."

Valeria nodded and entered the bathroom to get changed. She still wasn't comfortable undressing in front of Roberto.

As she was getting ready, Valeria pondered on how gentle Roberto was, and about the way he had shared his feelings. She didn't know how much he'd suffered in Italy, but she did know he'd at least taken the time to listen. The way he'd touched her had caused her to feel something, but it was something she didn't want.

She was here to make a better life for herself. She was completely unprepared to start a family and get too close to Roberto. She didn't want to risk rejection. Valeria thought about how a part of her had felt abandoned by her parents when they'd agreed to ship her off to Australia. It felt as if they couldn't wait to get rid of her. They'd never once asked her if she wanted to leave for Melbourne to get married. She wondered if Roberto could heal the part of her that felt abandoned, or whether he would reinforce those feelings.

Chapter 5

Seeing The Light

Valeria shook with nerves the next morning while eating a rasher of bacon with poached eggs. Roberto refused breakfast so he could meet up with Luca.

As he rushed out the door, Angela touched her arm with a reassuring smile. Grateful for Angela's kindness, Valeria smiled back, then rose from the table to clear the plates and wash the dishes while her sister-in-law got ready for work.

She tried not to think of what might be happening next door. It was frightening to think how Luca would respond. No doubt, he'd deny everything. Would Roberto believe him?

Valeria sat down, her hands clasped in her lap. She watched the clock in the kitchen and listened to the constant ticking. The minutes passed as if each was a lifetime. Turning to the window, the skies turned grey, casting little light on the day.

Reminding herself to breathe, she walked to the living room and drew open the curtain. The waiting was unbearable.

The clock ticked on. Sighing, she strolled over to the sofa, closed her eyes, and hoped this nightmare would end. She heard a voice, which brought her out of her thoughts.

"You're coming with me right now," Roberto said. His hands were shaking, and his face was white.

Her voice rose in alarm. "What happened?"

"You can't stay here by yourself."

Valeria shook her head. "But where do you want me to go?"

Roberto peered through the window. "Just for now you need to get out of here. Please."

Valeria's stomach turned. "Look, just tell me what happened."

Roberto softened. "He denied everything. He said that when you were going to the ladies' room, you passed by his table and invited him in for sex." Valeria stood as still as a statue. Her vision blurred. "The bastard called you a slut, and said he didn't want sex. He said he tried to set things straight; that he wouldn't touch you because you were married. He respected that."

Valeria closed her eyes, feeling sick. "Do you believe him?"

Roberto ignored the question. "Come on, let's go."

Valeria stood her ground. "I'm not letting him control my life. If I'm ever going to have my own business, I have to make a stand. I'm staying here."

Roberto's eyes darkened. "You can't stay home on your own. Either you come with me or I will not support you financially."

Valeria couldn't believe what she was hearing. If he didn't support her financially then she'd have to give up sewing. "I am not leaving this house." She fingered her throat. "Did you believe him this time?"

"Of course I didn't believe him. I got so angry— I punched him in the face— he's got a bloody nose. He probably won't go to work today. Which is why you can't stay here."

Valeria's cheeks warmed. "I'll be fine. I'll keep the doors locked. But I will not be driven from my home because of that creep."

Roberto sighed. "Why are you so damn stubborn—and why do you insist on being here, making yourself vulnerable to him?"

Valeria lifted her chin. "I don't need a man controlling me. I had enough of that from my father. I'm my own woman, and I can fight if I have to. Just go to work and leave me be. Please."

"Dammit, Valeria." His face turned bright red and his fists clenched. "You are coming with me now!" He grabbed her roughly by the shoulders. "I cannot protect you. Don't you see?"

Valeria shrugged him off and moved back, feeling enraged herself. What was going on with him, and why was he reacting this way?

Angela rushed out from her bedroom and laid a hand on Roberto's forearm. "Roberto, stop it."

Valeria's breathing accelerated. Feeling uneasy at Roberto's angry presence, she ran out of the living room and locked herself in the bedroom. Tears trickled down her face as she dropped onto the bed. Why had Roberto got so angry? Would he have hit her if Angela hadn't intervened? A cold fear settled in the pit of her stomach. Was he capable of violence just like Luca? Just like her father?

The bang of the front door slamming made her jump. A few moments later, she heard a knock on the bedroom door.

"Can I come in?" Angela asked. Valeria wiped her eyes and unlocked the door. "You know Roberto's just worried about you. He never would've hurt you." Valeria nodded but couldn't bring herself to speak.

"He does care about you. He was just—I guess, triggered and maybe feeling slightly rejected by you. You do keep

your distance and—I think you could get to know him."
Angela touched her on the shoulder. "Please. Give him a
chance. He's had some traumatic things happen back in
Italy, and today might have been too close to home. "When
there was no response, she dropped her hand to her side.
"Anyway, I'd better get to work. Just...think about it."

When the sound of the car engine had faded, Valeria got
up and locked the door.

Chapter 6

Close to the Edge

Roberto apologised to Valeria and promised to make it up to her by taking her to Williamstown Beach. He drove in his Valiant while Valeria peered through the window, observing the heavy congested traffic and wide lanes, while hearing the toot of horns. Her window was slightly open so she could enjoy the warm gust of autumn.

She missed the farm but was happy to be free of the familial responsibilities. At least here she appeared to have some measure of freedom.

Only time would tell if that was true. She was slowly getting to know Roberto, and so far, she knew so little about him.

As they arrived at the beach, swarms of people came out of weathered brick buildings that looked like restrooms, running over well-kept grass, and unloading supplies and picnic food near towering trees amidst the cool shade.

Roberto parked in a laneway close to the picnic areas under the trees. Valeria looked around and saw flies buzzing, seagulls perching on the pilings, and families playing soccer or bocce, which reminded her of her favourite pastime in Italy.

Roberto reached for her hand, surprising her. "Come on, let's go for a walk, *Bellissima.*"

Valeria nodded, her heart fluttering. "Along the beach?"

"Of course."

They strolled hand in hand, looking straight ahead as the sound of the crashing waves rolled over them. Cyclists and mothers pushing prams filled the footpath, along with young groups carrying radios, beach towels, and backpacks.

Roberto dropped onto a patch of sand along the shore and patted the ground beside him. She sat down near him and curled her legs underneath her. Roberto stared into her eyes as if peering into her soul. He took her hand again and held it to his cheek. This time, the flutter settled in her stomach.

He spoke first. "I really am sorry about the other day, Valeria. I guess I was just worried."

"Why? I can look after myself."

He frowned. "I only wanted to protect you, keep you safe."

"I'm glad you believe me now."

Roberto's body went still, almost statue-like. He faced the water's edge. "I should've realised how he was, but I was blind. Blind because he was always helpful, always there whenever we needed him. He did the right things."

Valeria nodded. "Does that mean you are no longer friends?"

"Not after what he did to you. I can never forgive him for that."

Valeria played with the fine granules of sand. She looked at Roberto differently. He seemed to truly care for her, and this worried her. She didn't want to risk getting close to him because in the end she'd most likely get hurt.

Roberto shifted. "You know, Luca once told me how much his father would beat him. How he used belts, whips, his fists, you name it, he used it on him. All because his mother left them. He took his anger and frustrations out on Luca. He was only eight when she left."

"I know. Angela told me." She took a deep breath. "It's pretty sad."

Roberto nodded, and then gazed into the distance. "He even said his father never wanted any of his friends over. He tortured his soul. It doesn't excuse what he did—but I understand where all that anger comes from."

"He needs help," Valeria said. Roberto turned back to her, eyes glistening. "Are you okay, Roberto? You seem like you're somewhere else."

Roberto wiped his eyes with the back of his hand. "I'm just remembering my dad, and how much I miss him. He died so young."

Valeria took his hand. "I'm sorry. I can't imagine losing a parent."

"It's okay." He managed a smile. "It was hard when my mum just shut down after his death. She was in shock for a while. She remarried—but that's another story."

"Tell me what happened?"

Roberto shook his head. "He was sick and we couldn't get him help in time."

Valeria gasped. "I am sorry, Roberto."

He swallowed. "Thanks." Valeria winced, her heart breaking at the idea of losing a parent at such a young age. Roberto changed the subject. "Why did your family arrange for you to come here? To marry me, I mean? My aunt never explained the reason."

Valeria felt cold. "I guess they wanted a better life for me here. They saw more opportunities." Her chest tightened for a moment. "I was the second oldest and my older sister was married." She paused. "I really miss them. My mum, brother and sisters."

"And your dad?"

Valeria shrugged. "Not as much. A little I guess."

"Why not?"

"He was just a hard man. Not the type to talk or listen."

Roberto said nothing. A few minutes later, a young man bumped into Roberto.

"Hey, watch it," he said.

The man turned around. "What did you say?"

"Nothing." Roberto turned away, but the man took a quick step forward and hit him in the face. Roberto stumbled backward, and the man hit him in the stomach, doubling him over. He threw a punch that caught his attacker squarely in the mouth. Blood sprayed across Roberto's knuckles. Then the stranger drove his shoulder into Roberto's chest, and the two men hit the ground in a flurry of punches. Valeria looked around and called to the passing herd, "Somebody, please do something. Stop this."

As she watched the brawl in horror, a young boy dropped something into her hand. It was a crumpled piece of paper. She ignored it and ran to Roberto as the young man delivered a final kick and loped away. Roberto staggered to his feet and ran after him.

Valeria started to follow, then remembered the note and unfolded it. It read:

I want you to tell Roberto you lied about me, and do it today. I have people watching and listening. If you don't, I have connections in Italy. Your family is as good as dead. If you tell Roberto the truth, he's as good as dead too.

Valeria read the note a few times. Her throat felt dry. This fight was a distraction, no doubt orchestrated by Luca. She couldn't fathom how she could lie to Roberto. Especially after all the times she'd tried to get him to believe her. Now she had to tell him it was a lie when it wasn't. A part of her wanted to tell Luca to go to hell. But, how could she take that risk? Her family's lives and Roberto's were at risk, and she didn't doubt Luca would hurt them if she failed to do as he said. He'd more than demonstrated his violent tendencies. She had to do this for Roberto and her family.

When Roberto returned, she slipped the note into the pocket of her dress. He was puffing. "Thank God he's gone."

"Are you okay?" She grabbed a tissue and wiped his mouth and nose, which was smeared with blood. "Did you know that man?"

Roberto shook his head. "Only some high-strung idiot with nothing better to do."

They walked back to the car and unloaded it. They took out a picnic basket, drinks, picnic blanket, and an ice cooler. Their hands brushed, and Roberto stroked her cheek, looking deeply into her eyes. He leaned in, lips pursed, about to kiss her. She felt a fizzing in her stomach and a heat below her stomach. Oh, how she wanted that kiss, but she could never have it. She moved back, out of reach. This could never happen. Luca would kill everyone she loved if they continued to turn against him.

Roberto's eyes darkened. "I am sorry."

Valeria felt dizzy, her breathing shallow. "It's fine."

Eventually, they sat down on the blanket and devoured the assorted cheeses, cold chicken, tomato salad, and frittata. It was a feast, but she barely enjoyed the food. She was thinking about her next words.

"Roberto, I need to tell you something."

"Hmm."

Valeria took a breath and thought about her family. She was doing this for her family and Roberto, so she had to be convincing.

"I—I— lied about Luca. None of it was true."

Roberto's face paled. "What?"

"What I said about him. None of that ever happened. I lied."

"What kind of a joke is this? You got me, okay."

Valeria's heart was breaking. "It's true. Luca never hurt me. I made it up so you'd feel sorry for me. I don't like the guy— so I made up the story to get him out of your life."

Roberto stared at her, his eyes narrowing. "You're lying, Valeria. I don't believe you."

Be convincing. She drew in a deep breath and looked him straight in the eye. "It's true. I made it all up."

Roberto shook his head, frowning. "No, that's ridiculous. I know he hurt you. I know."

Valeria didn't know how to convince him. "You really don't know me, do you? You don't know what I'm capable of." The look in his eyes made her chest ache. "I lied to get sympathy. I lied so he'd be out of our lives, and it worked."

Roberto turned away and started packing up the food and drinks. Without a word, he stepped into the car, waited for Valeria to enter, and drove off in a hurry. Valeria would've preferred his anger, but not the silence. The silence was much worse.

When they arrived home, Roberto left her alone and took a walk.

Valeria greeted Angela and Marco, who had returned from an appointment. She asked to use the telephone to ring her family, but there was no response. She tried several times over the course of a few hours, but there was still no answer. Her stomach ached and she bowed her head to hide her tears. What if Luca harmed her family? How would she cope? She did what he had asked but would that be enough?

Chapter 7

Danger Zone

A week later, Valeria stared through the window as Roberto drove out of his driveway when Luca stopped him. He swaggered towards Roberto, and the two men spent several minutes talking, smiling, and shaking hands. But something was off about Roberto. He appeared standoffish. Did he suspect she'd lied to him? Did he not trust Luca?

Eventually Luca left and returned to his house, and Roberto drove onto the road. Valeria closed her eyes and drew a hand through her hair. With Marco and Angela at work, Valeria was alone now. She thought she should probably do housework, or design a new dress for her business, but she couldn't seem to muster any enthusiasm for either project. Instead, she headed to her bedroom, fell onto the bed and stared up at the ceiling, tears trickling from the corners of her eyes.

She'd called her family four times with no answer. This worried her. Had Luca organised for someone to hurt them? There was no reason for that, since she'd done as he asked.

There had to be an explanation. She had to keep trying. She pushed herself off the bed and reached for the telephone, quelling a wave of anxiety. What if they still didn't answer?

She held the phone to her ear and counted the rings. Seventeen...eighteen...*Come on, pick up*...twenty...twenty-one. Abruptly, the ringing stopped and her mother's voice came on the line. *"Mama, come stai?"* She breathed a sigh of relief, her heart warming. Her mother was fine. *"Con uno amico? Fattoria?"* They chatted for a while, Valeria skirting the subject of relationships, her mother talking about how she and the rest of the family had spent the past week helping out a friend on her farm. Too soon, it was time to hang up. *"Ciao, Mamma. Io Ti voglio tanto bene."*

She laid the receiver gently in the cradle. With her family's absence explained, it felt like a great weight had been lifted from her chest. Now she could move on.

Valeria headed to the kitchen and made tea. She sat at the table, sipping her drink and thought of the day after

Williamstown beach. Roberto had confronted her after spending that night on the couch.

"How do you expect me to trust you now?"

She was shivering, her heart fragmented. "I'm sorry, but I don't want Luca in our lives, so I lied about him."

"Do you think this is the basis for a good marriage? Lies? Secrets? No trust?" Valeria said nothing, cringing inside. Roberto went on. "I really thought you had morals, a sense of decency, but obviously I was wrong. You're just manipulative and a plain liar."

She held his gaze as he berated her, a red wash creeping up his face. "I thought something was developing between us, but that's pointless now. I can't even look at you, and I don't trust you. I'll be sleeping on the couch from now on, at least until I can build another room for myself. As far as I'm concerned, you're only a woman who lives here."

Those words had cut deeply, but she couldn't blame him for feeling that way. For now, she had to play Luca's game. Roberto had said nothing to Marco and Angela, but for how long? Eventually, he'd have to tell them about her so-called lie.

She picked up her teacup and rinsed it in the sink, planning her day. She didn't intend to spend it moping over Roberto.

Valeria had spent the past week keeping busy. She was working on her English skills, and her new business. She had bought supplies with Angela's money and agreed to pay her back once the business was making a profit.

She now owned a black Singer sewing machine, a reconditioned overlocker, threads, needles, coloured pins, scissors, and a range of fabrics consisting of silks, satins, cotton, and woollen/polyesters.

She had approached several of Angela's friends who had put in their orders for blouses and pants. So far she had three orders and had drawn designs that fit in with the needs of her three new customers. Valeria was quickly learning how to create contemporary designs that blended in well with the fashions of the 1960s. Angela's friends were teaching her about the current trends.

Her hope was to build her business via word of mouth, which meant that once she completed all three outfits, her customers would spread the word within their own circle of friends and community. The completed outfits would be her walking advertisements for future business.

With the cup in its proper place, Valeria moved to the living room to work on her outfits. Roberto's distance unsettled her, but she had to keep the situation in perspective. If Luca had to come back into their lives, then so be it. She would do what she had to, to protect her family and herself.

She took out the sewing machine and added thread. As she was using her foot pedal and sewing machine to tackle a cross stitch, she thought about the type of buttons she would use for a casual blouse.

Losing focus, she accidentally pricked her finger under the sewing needle and cried out in pain. Blood trickled onto the cloth as she quickly stopped the machine, picked up scraps of material to wrap around her finger, and headed to the bathroom. She retrieved a bottle of disinfectant and dabbed it on her finger and secured it with a Band-Aid. It was only a superficial wound.

As she walked back to the living area, the rattling of a window jarred her. Were those footsteps in the next room? The hair on her arms lifted. The window was open, but she was sure it had been closed.

Quickly, she scanned the room but didn't notice anything out of the ordinary. She closed the window and shivered. Chills ran up and down her spine. When the phone in the kitchen rang, her heart leaped. She rushed for the phone.

"Listen, I spoke to Luca today and something didn't feel right. It just occurred to me now," Roberto said.

With growing concern, Valeria's hand shook. "What do you mean?"

"Well he wanted to be friends again, but he was cautious with me. Like he was hiding something." He paused. "Has he threatened you in any way?"

Valeria hesitated, tightening her grip on the phone. "Of course not. That's crazy."

"Valeria, listen. Why don't you take the bus to my work? I'll give you directions."

Valeria felt goose-bumps on her skin. "Okay." As he recited the directions, strong arms grabbed her from behind and twisted her hands behind her back. The phone clattered to the floor, and Valeria knew she was in trouble. She craned her neck over her shoulder and saw Luca grimacing as he fumbled to loop a rope around her wrists.

This time, she was ready. She pulled her head forward, then jerked it straight back, striking his chin with a loud crack. He stumbled and she pulled free, running towards the laundry.

His fist closed on a handful of hair and yanked her backward. A knee rammed into her lower back. Pain shot through her spine, and she fell to her knees with a strangled cry. For a moment, she couldn't breathe, couldn't move, couldn't see. Tears blurred her eyes, and she thought she might be paralysed.

Luca yanked her to her feet and snaked his arm around her throat. She clawed at his forearm gasping for breath, but his arm was like an iron bar. Her neck ached. Her chest burned. A wash of darkness obscured her vision, like a veil of grey across her eyes.

As if from a great distance, she was aware that he was dragging her towards the bedroom. Her fists thumped against his arms and sides. Then the pressure on her neck eased as he pushed her to the floor and tried to tie her hands to the leg of the bed.

Air. Sweet air. She sucked in a long breath and kicked him hard in the abdomen. He stumbled backward with a grunt, and let her go. She scrabbled to the bedside table, reaching for the clock radio. She could use it as a weapon.

She yanked it free of the wall and spun around to see Luca hovering over her with a crow bar. "Now do as I say or I'll hit you with this."

She stilled, hefting the clock and weighing her options. There weren't many.

She flung the clock.

He batted it aside with the crowbar as if it were paper, then drew back for another blow. It caught her on the temple, and she reeled backward, her arms and legs suddenly limp.

He pushed her roughly to the side of the bed and tied her hands to the leg of it. Once he was finished, he watched her menacingly.

"You stupid bitch. You destroyed my friendship with Roberto—the others too. All because you couldn't convince him you were lying. You'll pay for this."

Valeria tried not to show her terror. "Please Luca. I'm sorry. I didn't tell Roberto anything. I told him I lied, and now he's sleeping on the couch. Don't you see, he hates me? You broke us up. We don't even sleep in the same bedroom anymore."

Luca grinned. "Yeah, right. I'm not a fool and I'm not dancing to your tune."

"Why don't you believe me?"

He sighed. "I saw Roberto this morning. I could tell he was pretending, like he was playing along. You obviously weren't convincing enough."

Valeria met his gaze and her stomach sank at the chill in his eyes. "What are you planning to do?"

He licked his lips and rubbed his hands. "Well, I'll have my way with you then leave this dump of a place."

She wished she could knock the smirk off his face, but she would have to settle for stalling him until Roberto came. She was sure he would come for her.

"But you own your house, don't you?" she said. "How can you leave?"

He shook his head. "I've been renting the place." He glared. "Why should I stay in one place for too long? Three years is long enough." His eyes squinted. "Now shut the fuck up. I'm not here for intelligent conversation."

Valeria's heart was still racing. Her wrists were sore. Her shoulders were stretched to their limit. "What happened to you? Who hurt you so badly? Was it your mother, your father?"

She noticed a twitch. He turned away briefly.

"Shut up, I said." Luca placed his hands over his ears.

Valeria shook her head, blinking away tears. "I am not your parents, and I am not your ex-girlfriend, either."

He leaned down and slapped her hard. "I said, shut up."

Valeria ignored the pain. "Please don't do this. Let me go. If you want your way with me, then have me. I don't care anymore. I'm all yours, but please untie me."

"And why would I do that?"

Valeria paused to gain control of her roiling stomach. "Because then I'll be able to touch you."

"Just keep quiet. You talk too much." He barked an angry laugh. "You're not so tough anymore, are you?"

He left the room, and the front door slammed. Time passed but she lost track of time. Her mind cast back to the day her father had beaten her with his buckled belt. A woman in their village had told him she'd seen Valeria speaking to a boy in the street, when in fact, it had been another girl who resembled Valeria.

Despite her protests of innocence, her father had beaten her so hard that, without her sister's intervention, she would almost certainly have ended up in hospital. As it was, she ended up with cuts, bruises and grazes all over her body. Even when her father had discovered the truth, he hadn't even had the decency to apologise.

She had survived her father, and she would survive Luca too.

Valeria was alerted by a noise, and realised that Luca had returned with a sombre expression on his face. "We're leaving. I'll untie you but if you try anything, I'll have my crowbar right here. I won't be afraid to use it, okay, bitch?"

"Please don't call me that."

Luca ignored her and started untying the rope. "We're going to my house. Roberto won't be able to get in there, and even if he does, I'll be finished with you by then. I'll gladly put him in hospital."

Hesitantly, she stood up. Her knees buckled, and he pulled her back up and shoved her out of the room, towards the front door. It flew open, and Roberto charged in. He launched himself at Luca, and the two men tumbled on the floor, punching one another. The crowbar had fallen and Valeria rushed to grab it but she was too late. Luca's hand closed over it and snatched it up. She knew he planned to use it.

Valeria lurched toward him, but her feet felt like they were travelling in slow motion. Luca lifted the crowbar, and before either Valeria or Roberto could stop him, he brought it crashing down over Roberto's head.

Roberto slumped onto the floor and lay still.

Valeria screamed. "No! What have you done? What—what have—you—done?"

Luca blinked, staring at Roberto's limp body. The crowbar hung forgotten at his side. "He'll be fine."

"He doesn't look fine. He needs a doctor."

For a moment, Luca's expression softened as he continued to stare at Roberto's still body. He rubbed his temple hard and swore to himself. "Just move!" Luca ordered. He pushed Valeria out the door, and stumbled out after her. She turned her head back, again seeing Roberto's still, crumpled frame on the floor. What if he was dead? It would all be her fault. She needed to get help.

Once they reached Luca's house, he unlocked the door and shoved her inside. Valeria noticed a living area with strewn newspapers over crumb-filled floors, ashtrays overflowing with cigarettes, and a pungent odour like that of dead animals.

The furnishing was bland and weathered and the television looked old. The bedroom was much worse, with plates of food on the bedside table, a small beer bottle, and an unmade bed with lumps and a soiled quilt. There was an antique wardrobe that looked similar to one from back home. The bed was filled with assorted crumbs of food, while ashtrays lined the floor. Drawn curtains let a hint of sunlight seep through.

Luca, still holding on to the crowbar, ordered her, "Now get on the bed and take off your clothes."

Valeria hyperventilated and clutched her throat. Black spots appeared in her vision, but she had to mask it all. She had to put on a show so she could save Roberto and leave this filthy place. She forced a flirtatious tone into her voice. "I'd much rather you take them off me."

"Fine." With the crowbar in his left hand, he forced her onto the bed and lay on top of her. He kissed her roughly and guided Valeria's hand towards his penis. She felt nauseated but had no choice. There was no doubt in her mind he had the capacity to kill. As she touched him, he lifted her skirt and stroked her abdomen. His hand slid lower. Before he could get any further, she moved his hand up towards her cheek and kissed him.

Suddenly, she bit him hard on his lower lip.

"Aaah, you bitch." He slapped her, but it was a glancing blow. Ignoring the pain, she slithered out of his grip, twisted the crowbar out of his weakened grasp, and hit him on the legs as hard as she could muster.

He shrank away, shielding his legs with his hands. "You'll pay for this." He lunged across the bed and punched her hard in the face. Blood streamed from her nose. He pulled her to him by the hair, and Valeria screamed as he threw her on the floor. She lost sight of the crowbar but snatched an empty beer bottle that had rolled beneath the bed.

She knew he would kill her if she angered him enough. She didn't intend to let him. She climbed to her feet, the bottle behind her back.

He was screaming something at her, but she couldn't make out the words. Maybe they weren't even words anymore. With a malevolent grin, he reached down by the other side of the bed and came up with the crowbar.

She swung the bottle at his temple as hard as she could. It hit with a sickening crack, and he stumbled back, blinking rapidly. His eyes rolled back, and he fell limp onto the carpeted floor.

Valeria swayed on her feet, then steadied herself and inched closer, feeling queasy. She hadn't meant for him to die. On the other hand, she didn't want him to wake up any time soon either.

Brushing away those thoughts, she noticed the telephone on the bedside table. Using what she'd learned in English class, she dialled the operator and asked for an ambulance and the local police. She spoke in broken English to the operator. "Two mans hurt. Need police—and ambulance." She gave the operator the addresses.

Valeria walked back to her house and stayed with Roberto. Her heart ached at seeing Roberto again. She fell down to her knees and rested beside him, stroking his head. So many thoughts and emotions ran through her, and she cursed herself for bringing him into this situation. He had risked his life for her. A strange emotion ran through her as she realised she couldn't live without him.

After what seemed like hours, the police and ambulance staff were at the door. They entered Roberto's house, assessing the scene before them. From what the police were saying, she understood that they were arranging an Italian interpreter for her statement. After the ambulance staff checked his vitals and lay him on a stretcher, Valeria made her way into the ambulance with Roberto as they took him to the Royal Melbourne Hospital.

As she was getting into the ambulance, she turned at the sound of Luca's ranting and raving at the policemen. He was alive, and she felt relieved she hadn't killed him. He was in handcuffs, pushed forward by policemen into a police car. He stumbled a few times but luckily he didn't see her.

Chapter 8

New Journey

Valeria arrived at the hospital and sat in the waiting area. Her stomach was knotted with worry as she wondered whether Roberto would make it. What if he died on her? How could she cope with the guilt of putting him in harm's way?

The doctor arrived with a nurse who spoke Italian. She explained to Valeria that she would be acting as an interpreter.

"How is he?" Valeria asked.

"We performed the surgery and managed to control the bleeding in his brain. He should make a full recovery."

Valeria breathed a sigh of relief. "Can I see him?" The nurse spoke to the doctor and then nodded in response. "Thank you," Valeria said.

The nurse told her about the police statement, and that she would be her interpreter once they arrived.

Valeria nodded. "Please call me once they get here."

She hurried to Roberto's ward and tiptoed into his bed. A bandage covered one side of his head, and he was connected to a machine that monitored his oxygen levels. His eyes were closed, but when she approached the bed, his eyelids fluttered open. He gave her a sleepy smile.

"How are you?" Valeria asked.

"A little drowsy from the medication but I'll be okay."

"Good." She held his hand. "You gave me such a fright."

"Are you—okay?" he asked groggily.

"I'm fine."

"And Luca?"

"He's been arrested. The police will want to talk to you later, to get your statement. When you're up to it."

He nodded. "Valeria. I—I'm sorry. I tried to help but I failed you. So sorry."

"Don't be silly. You cared enough to come home. You were obviously worried about me."

He gave her a small grin. "Of course I was worried. I do care, you know." After a moment, he added, "He threatened you, didn't he?"

Valeria looked away. "He threatened to hurt my family, and you, so I had to lie. Luca did hurt me. A few times."

He nodded. "I suspected as much. I know you. Valeria, I..." His voice trailed off as he drifted into sleep.

"You what?" she asked silently.

Valeria sat by his side and watched him sleep, wondering what she would have done if he'd died. Perhaps now they could live their lives free of Luca.

Valeria turned to find Angela and Marco enter the ward. They hugged Valeria and came to stand by Roberto's side.

Lowering her voice so as not to wake her sleeping brother, Angela asked, "Is he going to be okay?"

"He's going to be fine. Only sleepy from the medication."

Marco asked, "What happened today?"

"Luca happened," Valeria said. She explained the whole story and saw them both wince. "Roberto will be fine now, and Luca will hopefully pay for his sins."

Angela embraced her warmly. "I'm sorry for not believing you at first. I never imagined he was like this. He was always there supporting us. I never would've thought."

"I'm sorry too," Marco said. "But he'd been a friend to us and helped us over the years when we needed it. We never realised he was sick like this."

Valeria forced a reassuring smile." These kinds of people are skilled at wearing a mask and fooling people. I'm sure he still cared about you guys. He just needs help."

"Anyway, from now on, we'll believe whatever you tell us," Angela said.

Valeria raised an eyebrow and, with a mischievous grin, said, "I could lie."

Angela and Marco both laughed.

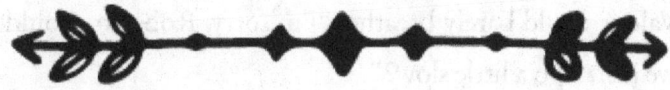

Two weeks later, Roberto and Valeria were returning from dinner at a local restaurant. It was the second time in three days they had gone out as a couple. Roberto wished to court her, and Valeria had agreed.

As they got to know each other after sharing the traumatic situation with Luca, feelings had started to develop between them, which caught them both by surprise.

When they arrived home, they entered the bedroom. Roberto stared into Valeria's eyes as he pulled her close to him and stroked her arm. Gently, he kissed her on the lips. She was giddy with emotion.

"I love you, Valeria," He murmured.

"I love you too, Roberto."

He tugged her towards the bed. "Why don't I show you how much I love you?"

Luca's leering face flashed through her mind, and a bolt of fear shot through her. But she drew in a long breath and blew it out. This was not Luca. This was Roberto, the man she loved. "I'd like that," she said softly.

Gently and slowly, he undressed her and then himself. Valeria could barely breathe. "I'm sorry, Roberto. Could we just. . .go a little slow?"

"It's okay. Relax and we'll go at your pace." He kissed her gently again and caressed her cheek. She shivered, this time with pleasure. She'd never felt anything like this before.

She allowed Roberto to take the lead as he stroked her in all the right places. She was aroused, and when she was ready, they eventually made love. Valeria experienced pain but mostly pleasure, with the certainty she would always love Roberto.

Chapter 9

A Walk to the Other Side

1966

Nine months later, Valeria had a baby girl named Maria. She named her after Roberto's mother.

The hospital sent her home two days after the birth, and she'd felt fine at the time. She'd had a difficult pregnancy with labour lasting almost twenty-four hours. She'd never experienced such pain but the reward was worth it.

A few days after arriving from the hospital, Valeria lay in bed with Roberto, who was sleeping. Maria slept soundly in her bassinette. She was lying awake in bed thinking about her pregnancy and how she wasn't ready to be a mother at nineteen years of age. She hadn't had her business for long and wanted time to settle in a new country. Her English was improving every day, and she was grateful the language would help with her career.

She had been shocked at the news of her pregnancy when she was tested at the local clinic. Roberto had encouraged her, giving her the confidence she needed to be a new mother, but the self-doubt lingered. However, with help from Roberto, Angela, Marco and her new friends, Valeria slowly came to terms with the pregnancy.

After Maria's birth, she felt such a surge of joy and love that no amount of words could ever describe. She realised that all she needed to raise her daughter was love, and that she would be fine. She had all the required domestic skills and was not alone.

As Valeria's heart warmed at fond memories, she suddenly felt sick in the stomach. The nausea sharpened into a stabbing pain that caused her to moan. Her head began to throb, and she pressed hard on her temple. Another moan escaped her. Roberto stirred, then became wide awake.

"What's wrong? "he asked.

"I've got such a bad headache. My stomach's killing me too."

"I'll get you a tablet." He rose from the bed and headed towards the kitchen.

As Roberto started toward the door, a wet warmth gushed down Valeria's thigh. The sheets were filled with blood. She felt light-headed, drifting in and out of consciousness. A gentle hand tugged at her. "Valeria—Valeria, oh my God! You're bleeding."

Valeria could barely hear Roberto as he rushed out of the room and called out to the others. She was barely conscious when he returned and carried her outside to his car.

"The baby," Valeria said.

"Don't worry. Angela will stay here with her. We're taking you to the hospital."

Valeria felt dizzy. She felt him lift her up. The world went black, and she felt nothing else.

When she woke up, she realised she wasn't at home in her own bed, but in another place filled with noise in the background. She heard scurrying feet and muffled voices. Where was she? Whose bed was she in? She glanced around groggily and saw an old woman beside her. She was wearing an old-fashioned white nun's hat. In the light from the windows, she looked suffused in gold.

Valeria had never seen a woman look so lovingly powerful through her presence alone, and it evoked a strong feeling of rightness and love in her. This woman's energy was so strong, Valeria could barely breathe.

The woman approached and stroked her on the face. "*Povera ragazza*," she said in Italian. Sitting by Valeria's side for a few minutes, she stood up and walked away.

Valeria found she couldn't speak. She felt weightless and detached from her surroundings. Everything around her looked blurry and faded, but she got a sense of euphoria and pure love inside her. Was this what it felt like to be dead? If this was what heaven was like, then it wasn't too bad.

She was sure Roberto would take good care of their daughter. They would be okay without her. Of course, they had Angela to help. Besides, Valeria knew Roberto would find someone else to take her place. She wanted that for him. He deserved to have a loving, generous woman beside him.

She lay back against the pillow and drifted. Sometime later, another woman came into the room. This woman wore a striped uniform but no funny-looking hat. Where had the other woman gone?

"How are you feeling, Valeria?" the woman said in Italian.

"What?" Valeria blinked as the room came suddenly into focus. The air smelled sharp, like bleach and antiseptic. "Where am I?"

"You're in the hospital."

She struggled to lift her body. "Why?"

"You were brought in by your husband." The nurse picked up her chart and scribbled something on it. "You were bleeding heavily. We managed to control the infection you caught after you had your baby. I believe you were taken home too soon, and your body couldn't cope."

"So—so—I'm not dead? I'm not in heaven?"

The woman laughed. "No, you're not in heaven. You're very much alive—and I'll be your nurse for today."

"But what about the other nurse that was here before? She was wearing an old nun's hat, almost like a sun hat. She looked quite old too. Where is she?"

The nurse knit her brows. "I'm sorry, but there's no nurse here that looks like that."

The nurse left, and Valeria felt cold all over. What was going on here? She was sure the woman was real. But, there was that strange feeling of something unreal about her. Was she an angel reassuring her that she'd be fine? Valeria could have died, and maybe at the time, she had been close to death. She had certainly felt weightless, like being in another dimension.

She realised now that the woman had been sent here to give her the message it wasn't her time to go yet. It was an amazing thought. She would hold this situation close to her heart.

Valeria's reverie broke when Roberto arrived and kissed her warmly on the lips. He brought Maria in the pram and lifted her out so that Valeria could hold her in bed. Valeria stroked her daughter's cheek and kissed her lovingly.

"How are you feeling, darling?"

Valeria recounted her experience, and Roberto smiled. "You have an angel by your side."

Valeria's heart warmed. It had felt surreal and magical. "How are you?"

"I'm fine, but missing you." He winked. "Anyway, the doctors say you don't have to stay more than a few days."

"That's great. I miss you all so much."

"And we've missed you too. More than you know." Roberto lay beside her on the bed and they gently embraced.

Valeria looked back over the past year of her life and realised she'd achieved quite a few things. She thought about how her business was slowly building and how she would eventually need another seamstress to keep up with the increasing orders. Angela was helping out on a part-time basis. Roberto was also starting his carpentry apprenticeship soon, and Valeria was planning to get her driver's licence.

Looking into the faces of her husband and the tiny person they'd made together, she realised that Australia was her new, cherished life, a life for which she would be forever grateful.

Reviews are gold to authors and allow Lucy to keep writing. If you enjoyed the story, please consider rating and reviewing it here: https://books2read.com/u/mqqwZm

Read more books in the Italian Family Series:
(Roberto's Childhood Story) *The Beauty of Tears*:
https://books2read.com/u/bpqwk3

(Valeria's Childhood Story) *Dancing In The Rain*:
https://books2read.com/u/bOr7LA

(Elena's Story) *A Life By Design*:
https://books2read.com/u/3J8ene

ABOUT THE AUTHOR

Lucy Appadoo is a prolific reader and author of the Friends In Crisis and Women Of Strength Series. After a childhood spent reading and imagining escapist worlds, Lucy has put her imagination into stories. Her work as a rehabilitation counsellor, and former work as a counsellor in private practice, have led to an interest in writing inspirational stories about authentic, driven women who manage adversity with strength and heart. She writes in the genres of romantic suspense/thrillers with significant life themes and contemporary romance.

Lucy's interests include researching crime stories and news to inspire her work, watching crime thrillers and suspenseful movies, travel, exercising, reading for entertainment or knowledge, meditation, and spending time with friends and family. She also appreciates her Italian background and culture, which has inspired her to write imaginative stories about her parents' childhoods, leading to The Italian Family Series novels.

Check out Lucy's website and sign up for a free suspenseful book:

https://www.lucyappadooauthor.com.au

ALSO BY LUCY APPADOO

Web Of Lies (Book 3):
https://books2read.com/u/3JXazE
Love-Obsessed (Book 4):
https://books2read.com/u/4jPKGX

The Hearts Series - Romantic Suspense

Rising Hearts (Book 1):
https://books2read.com/u/mZwpoE
Forbidden Hearts (Book 2):
https://books2read.com/u/bQBKr7
Kindred Hearts (Book 3):
https://books2read.com/u/4AJKQK
Broken Hearts (prequel to Forbidden Hearts):
https://books2read.com/u/mgrnOD

Short Story Thrillers

Evening Interrupted:
https://books2read.com/u/3yZDjZ
The Dreamcatcher: https://books2read.com/u/bzaLxn
Red Flags: https://books2read.com/u/bWZ9W1
Collection of Short Story Thrillers:
https://books2read.com/u/bP5vwj

The Italian Family Series - Coming of Age Family Drama/Romance

The Beauty of Tears: https://books2read.com/u/bpqwk3

Dancing in the Rain:
https://books2read.com/u/bOr7LA

A Life By Design: https://books2read.com/u/3J8ene

NON-FICTION
Grief & Loss

Moving Beyond Grief - How To Shift From Grief & Loss to Joy & Peace: https://books2read.com/u/mVNzDA

Stress Management & Anxiety

Holistic Spiritual and Mental Health - Building Resilience and Creativity by Conquering Anxiety and Managing Stress: https://books2read.com/u/47kG8A

Career Guidance

Your Holistic Career Path - Create Career Change, Satisfaction, and Work/Life Balance: https://books2read.com/u/bzYDz4